John Lennon   Jean Jullien

IMAGINE

This book is very special to me. The words were written by my husband, John,
and it makes me so happy to see them illustrated in this beautiful book.
He wrote "Imagine" as a song calling for peace around the
world. Today, we need peace more than ever, so I think
his words are still very important.

Everybody wants to feel happy and to feel safe. And we
can all help make the world a better place in our own way.
We should always keep love in our hearts, and look after one another. We
should always share what we have, and we should stand up for people who
are not being treated fairly.

And it's important that we treat everyone like that, not just our family and our
friends. We should treat everybody the same, no matter where they are from or
if they speak a different language. After all, the pigeon in this book welcomes
all the other birds, whatever color of feathers or shape of beak they have.

By doing this, we can all help to make a difference every day. Every small,
good thing that we do can help change the world for the better. You can do it,
I can do it, we all can do it.

Imagine. Together we can make peace happen. Then the world truly will live
as one.

—Yoko Ono Lennon

CLARION BOOKS
Houghton Mifflin Harcourt
Boston   New York

Published in partnership with Amnesty International

Imagine there's no heaven.

It's easy if
you try.

No hell below us.

Above us, only
sky.

Imagine all the people
living for today.

It isn't hard to do.

Nothing to kill or die for,

and no religion too.

Imagine all the people
living life in **peace.**

You may say I'm a dreamer,

but I'm not the only one.

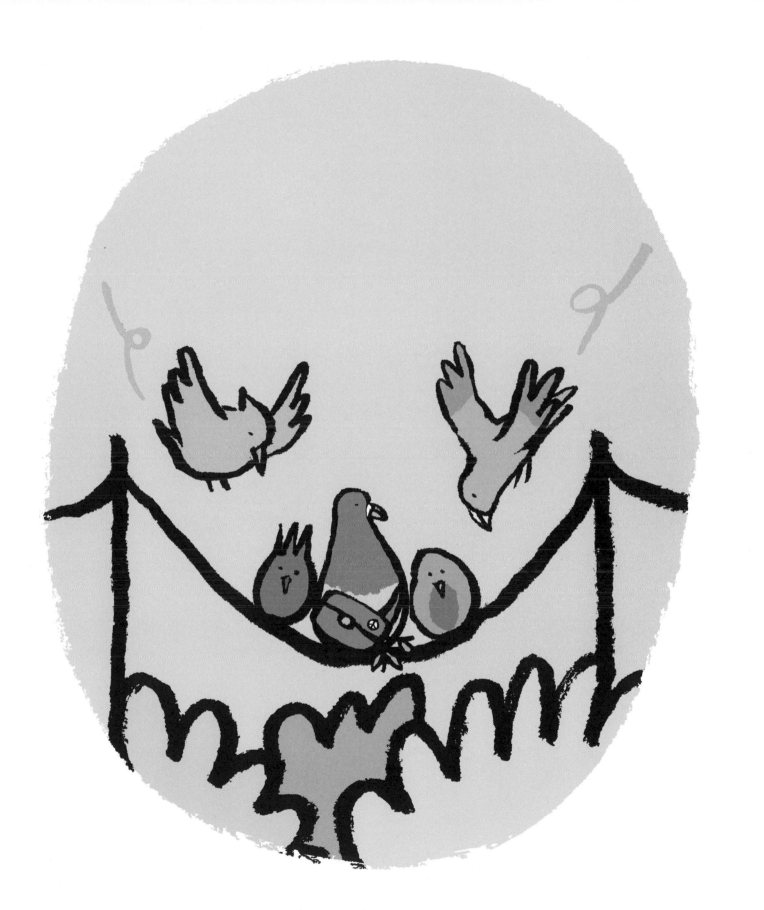

I hope some day you'll join us,

and the world will
be as **one**.

Imagine no
possessions.

I wonder if you can.

No need for
greed or hunger.

A **brotherhood**
of man.

Imagine all
the people **sharing**
all the world.

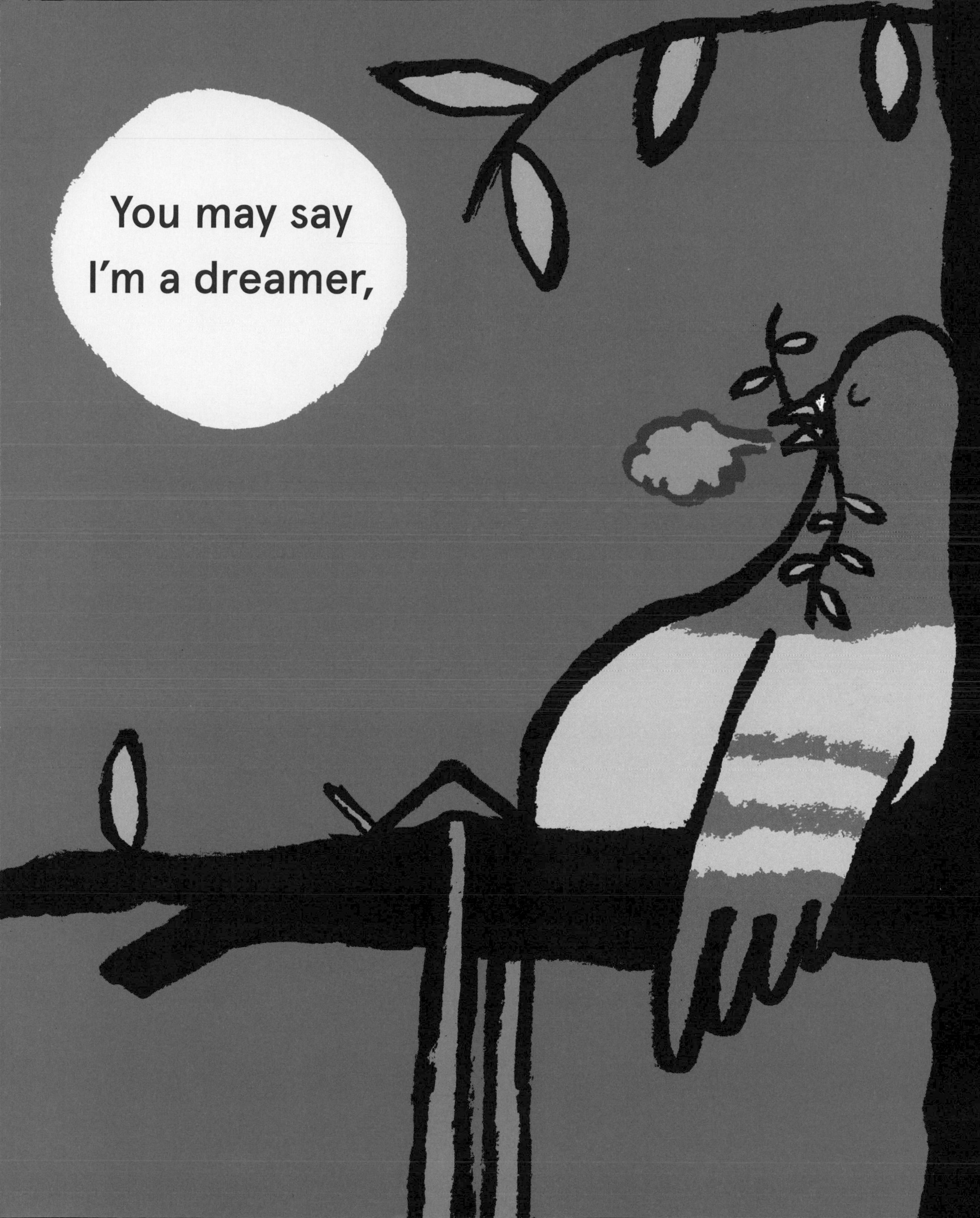

You may say
I'm a dreamer,

but I'm not the only one.

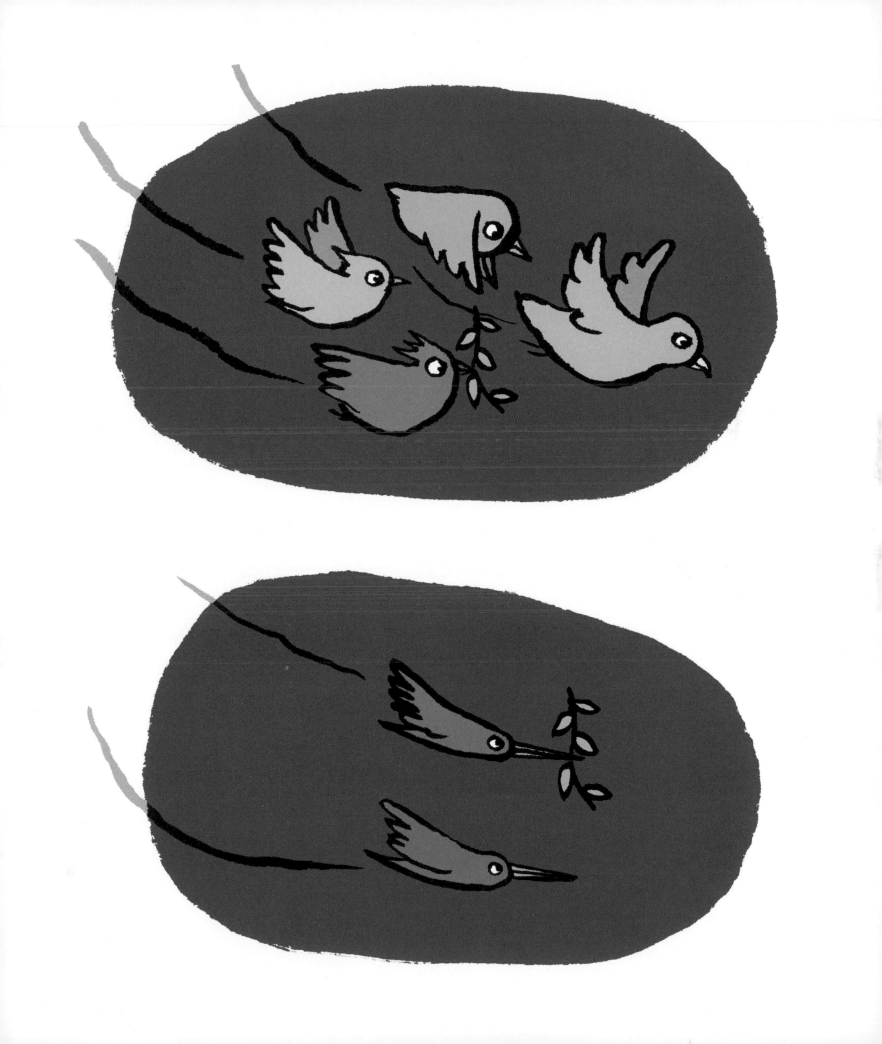

I **hope** some day
you'll join us,

And the world will
live as one.

AFTERWORD

This book is about peace, which helps us enjoy a happy and safe life. For peace to flourish, we need to treat everyone kindly, equally, and fairly.

We also need to look after some precious freedoms called human rights, which protect all of us. Every baby, child, and grownup in the world has human rights. They were first proclaimed in 1948, when the world said "never again" to the horrors of the Second World War. It was then that the Universal Declaration of Human Rights was born. Human rights are rooted in values such as fairness, truth, equality, love, home, and safety. They are part of what make us human and no one should take them away from us.

Amnesty International works to protect our human rights. We want to say a big thank-you to Jean Jullien for his beautiful pictures and to Yoko Ono Lennon for her kindness in letting us use John Lennon's wonderful words in this book.

We want to thank you, too, for helping to make the world a better place.

Thank you.

Amnesty International

Join the human rights movement; become an Amnesty International member today.
In the U.S., go to: **www.amnestyusa.org/donate**; *in Canada,* **www.amnesty.ca/donate**.

Amnesty International USA
5 Penn Plaza
New York, NY 10001
Tel: 1.800.AMNESTY
www.amnestyusa.org

Amnesty International Canada
312 Laurier Avenue East
Ottawa, ON K1N 1H9
Tel: 1.800.266.3789
www.amnesty.ca

CLARION BOOKS
3 Park Avenue, New York, New York 10016

"Imagine" written by John Lennon © 1971 by Lennon Music, renewed 1998
Illustrations © 2017 by Jean Jullien

Foreword © 2017 by Yoko Ono Lennon
Afterword © 2017 by Amnesty International UK Section

First published in the United States of America in 2017 by Houghton Mifflin Harcourt Publishing Company in association with Amnesty International.

First published in the United Kingdom in 2017 by Frances Lincoln Children's Books, an imprint of The Quarto Group, in association with Amnesty International.

All rights reserved. For information about permission to reproduce selections from this book, write to trade.permissions@hmhco.com or to Permissions, Houghton Mifflin Harcourt Publishing Company, 3 Park Avenue, 19th Floor, New York, New York 10016.

Clarion Books is an imprint of Houghton Mifflin Harcourt Publishing Company.

www.hmhco.com

The illustrations in this book were done in brush and ink, then colored digitally. The text was set in Apercu.

Library of Congress Cataloging-in-Publication Data is available.
ISBN: 978-1-328-80865-3

Manufactured in China
10 9 8 7 6 5 4 3 2 1
4500652895